A Lullaby of Love for

Amelia

By Suzanne Marshall

LiveWellMedia.com

ISBN: 9798840442241

This book is dedicated to

AMELIA

who is loved very much!

Amelia,

are you ready to give thanks tonight

for all that is peaceful, warm and bright?

Amelia,

as the Deer plays guitar with glee,

we give thanks for you and me,

and our time together in harmony.

I AM
THANKFUL

Amelia,

as the Hippo plays the violin,

we give thanks for giggles and grins,

and belly laughs from deep within.

Amelia,

as the Owl drums like a pro,

we give thanks for adventures

that help us grow,

even "oopsy-daisies"

and "uh-ohs."

Amelia,

as the Giraffe softly sings,

we give thanks for everything,

like smooches from pooches,

and butterfly wings.

Amelia,

as the Eagle plays the harp,

we give thanks for your big heart;

you are brave and you are smart.

Amelia,

as the Badger plays clarinet,

we give thanks for every breath,

like each deep breath

that helps us rest.

Amelia,

as the Antelope plays maracas,

we give thanks for cuddles and hugs,

and all that is cozy,

comfy and snug.

Amelia,

as the Elk plays the cello,

we give thanks that you are mellow,

like a spongy, sweet marshmallow.

Amelia,

as the Bunny plays the violin,

we give thanks for family and friends,

and love that never,

ever ends.

Amelia,

as the Fox plays the flute,

I give thanks that you are YOU.

You are loved and loving too.

Amelia,

as the Bear plays the sax,

as you sleep, as you relax,

I LOVE YOU

to the moon and back.

GOODNIGHT
AMELIA

Credits

Special thanks to my family and to my dear friends Hannah and Rachel Roeder. All illustrations have been edited by the author. Musical animals and hot-air balloon: © ddraw (freepik). Main cat, cat friend & sleeping kitty: © dazdraperma (fotosearch). Puppy: yayayoyo (fotosearch). Moon and lantern: © zzve (fotosearch). Floral ladder: © colematt (fotosearch). Additional elements were curated from freepik.

About the Author

An honors graduate of Smith College, Suzanne Marshall writes to inspire, engage and empower children. Learn more about Suzanne and her books at **LiveWellMedia.com**. *(Photo: Suzanne & Abby Underdog)*

More Personalized Books from LiveWellMedia.com

Personalize with any name

I Love You to the Moon
SOPHIA
by Suzanne Marshall

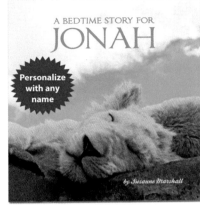

A BEDTIME STORY FOR
JONAH

Personalize with any name

by Suzanne Marshall

Personalize with Any Name

Love You Forever
ABBY
by Suzanne Marshall

Personalize with Any Name

Birthday Wishes for
ABBY
by Suzanne Marshall

Personalize with Any Name

Celebrating
RACHEL
by Suzanne Marshall

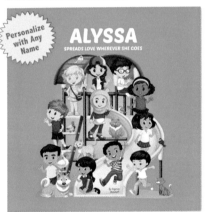

Personalize with Any Name

ALYSSA
SPREADS LOVE WHEREVER SHE GOES
by Suzanne Marshall

Personalize with any Name

Positive Affirmations for
RACHEL

Personalized Coloring Book
by Suzanne Marshall

Personalize with any Name

YOU ARE LOVED

MALCOLM

Personalized Coloring Book
by Suzanne Marshall

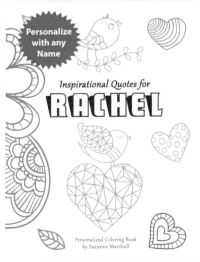

Personalize with any Name

Inspirational Quotes for
RACHEL

Personalized Coloring Book
by Suzanne Marshall

Made in the USA
Las Vegas, NV
24 February 2024

86246862R00019